Greedy Cat
and the
Birthday Cake

Joy Cowley
illustrated by Robyn Belton

Learning Media

Chapter 1

Greedy Cat stopped on the path. His nose twitched, and his whiskers sprang up. He could smell chocolate!

Up the steps he ran. Plop! He was through the cat door and into the kitchen. "Chocolate! Chocolate!" he called to Katie.

He rubbed against her legs. "I want
chocolate!"

To Katie, this sounded like "Purr, meow,
purr, meow!" So she took no notice. She
went on mixing chocolate and sugar and
butter to make a birthday cake for Mom.
Greedy Cat put out his pink tongue and
tasted the air. "Chocolate!" he squealed,
clawing at Katie's jeans.

She pushed him away. "What are you yowling about?" she asked. "I fed you. Look! You've still got meat and cat snacks in your dish."

Greedy Cat sniffed at his dish. "I don't feel like meat, and I don't want cat snacks!" He yowled as loudly as he could, "Chocolate! Chocolate! I need chocolate!"

"I can't stand that yowling!" said Katie.
"Out you go!"

Chapter 2

Katie spread the chocolate cake mix into the baking pan. Greedy Cat was on the back porch with his nose beside the gap under the kitchen door.

When the cake went into the oven, the
smell of chocolate grew stronger. It
curled out of the oven, under the door,
and right up to Greedy Cat's nose.
He wanted to get in, but Katie had
locked the cat door.

When Dad came home, Greedy Cat was on the doorstep. He rushed inside between Dad's feet. "Hey!" said Dad. "Why don't you use your own door?"

"Oh, that cat!" said Katie. "I locked him out. He was yowling at me while I was making Mom's birthday cake. What a pest!"

"How did the cake turn out?" asked Dad.

"Just great!" said Katie. "A chocolate layer cake with chocolate cream frosting and a pink candle on top." Then she whispered, "I've hidden it in a safe place until Mom's party tomorrow."

Greedy Cat rubbed against Katie's legs. The smell of chocolate was still in the air, and it made his stomach rumble. He meowed in his cutest voice, "Chocolate?"

"Are you hungry?" asked Katie.

Greedy Cat purred.

"Then eat your supper," said Katie, and she gave him his dish of cat snacks.

Chapter 3

In that house, food smells came and went. But the chocolate smell stayed. Even late at night, when every room was dark, the smell of chocolate was everywhere. To Greedy Cat, it was the best smell in the world.

He walked softly from room to room, trying to find where the smell started.

In the kitchen, the lights on the stove blinked like red eyes. Greedy Cat sniffed from the fridge to the stove and from the stove to the table. Chocolate had been there, but it was not there now.

In the living room, he could smell
flowers, magazines, and old sneakers. He
jumped up on the table and looked at the
goldfish bowl. The fish was interesting,
but it was not made of chocolate.

Mom and Dad slept in the big bedroom.
Greedy Cat crept past the exercise
machine, past Dad's baseball cap, and
past Mom's jacket. He jumped onto the
bed. Mom and Dad both snored, but
their breath did not smell of chocolate.

Four fat, fluffy feet padded down the hall to Katie's room. One paw lifted to push open the door. Creak, c-r-e-a-k. Katie did not wake up. Greedy Cat put his pink nose in the air and sniffed. This was it! This was the place of chocolate!

He ran across the rug, following the
smell to Katie's closet. He squeezed
through. In the closet was a tray. On the
tray was a cloth. Under the cloth was …

… the chocolate cake!

Chapter 4

The next morning, Greedy Cat hid in the oak tree. Katie stood on the back porch and yelled and cried. Mom tried not to laugh.

"A whole cake!" Katie shouted at the oak tree. "You're a great, greedy gobble-guts! How could you do it?"

"That cat stretches like a balloon," said Dad. "One day he'll burst."

Katie's closet was a mess. There were cake crumbs everywhere. Chocolate pawprints covered the bedroom floor. At the end of the bed was a pink candle … with toothmarks in it.

"It was going to be a surprise!" cried Katie.

Mom wiped the tears from Katie's eyes. "It is a surprise," she said. "It's the biggest surprise I've had in years."

"I'll make you another cake," Katie said to her mom.

"And this time," said Dad, "we'll lock Greedy Cat in the laundry room."

But Greedy Cat stayed in the oak tree. He did not even get excited when the smell of chocolate drifted up from the kitchen again. To tell the truth, he was feeling quite sick!

Chapter 5

That night, the table was set for Mom's birthday. In the middle of the table, there was a birthday card from Katie. Beside the card was a chocolate layer cake with chocolate cream frosting and a new blue candle.

Greedy Cat knew something was happening. He sat outside the locked cat door. "Let me in!" he cried. "Let me in!"

"Greedy Cat is yowling," said Katie. "Can he come in?"

"Do you think he's learned a lesson?" said Dad.

Katie laughed. "No. He'll never learn. But we can't have a party without Greedy Cat. He's one of the family."

Dad unlocked the cat door, and Greedy Cat rushed inside. He purred against their legs.

Katie tickled him under the chin. "Poor old Greedy Cat. He doesn't have his own birthday. Maybe that's why he ate Mom's cake."

"Don't you believe it," said Dad. "He ate it because he's greedy."

"Well," said Mom, "I don't mind if he shares my birthday. But he doesn't get a crumb of this cake."

Greedy Cat sniffed. He was hungry again, but he didn't want chocolate cake. He didn't know what he wanted. He tried to jump onto Katie's lap, but there was not enough room. He slid back onto the floor. "Meow?"

Katie looked at him. "I've got a great idea," she said, and she ran into the kitchen.

After a while, she came back with a birthday cake that was perfect for a cat. It was made of canned meat with some cat snacks on top. And right in the middle, there was a sardine, sticking up like a candle!

Katie sang, "Happy birthday to you.
Happy birthday to you.
Happy birthday,
dear Greedy Cat.
Happy birthday
to you."

Greedy Cat ran to his dish. Now, he
knew what he wanted. "Gobble! Gobble!
Gobble!" His cat cake *was*
purr-fect!

Greedy Cat curled up on the mat and closed his eyes. Chocolate cake was nice, but nothing was better than cat meat and cat snacks.